The Very Worried Sparrow

A Lion Children's Book
an imprint of
Lion Hudson plc
Mayfield House, 256 Banbury Road,
Oxford OX2 7DH, England
www.lionhudson.com

ISBN-13: 978 0 7459 4938 3
ISBN-10: 0 7459 4938 X

First edition 2006
10 9 8 7 6 5 4 3 2 1 0

Typeset in 18/30 BlockheadUnplugged
Printed and bound in China

To Micah and the next
generation M.D.

To my very best friend
Shannon with love G.H.

Meryl
Doney

ILLUSTRATED BY
Gaby
Hansen

The Very Worried Sparrow

LION
CHILDREN'S

There was once a Very Worried Sparrow.
All the other baby birds looked up at the bright
blue sky and sang, 'Cheep, cheep! Cheep, cheep!'
But not the Very Worried Sparrow. 'Meep,
meep,' he said in a very little voice.

The first thing he worried about was food.

'Oh dear!' he thought. 'I'm so hungry.
Whatever am I going to eat?'

Suddenly, there was Mother, with a fat,
juicy caterpillar for each baby bird.

One day, Father gathered the little
sparrows around him.

'I think it is time you
learned to fly,' he said.
'Open your wings and flap.'

'Wheeeeeee, this is lovely,'
called the sparrows.

'Meep, meep,' said the Very Worried Sparrow.

'I don't dare.'

He was so scared he lost his
balance, toppled off the branch...
flipped... and flapped... and flew!

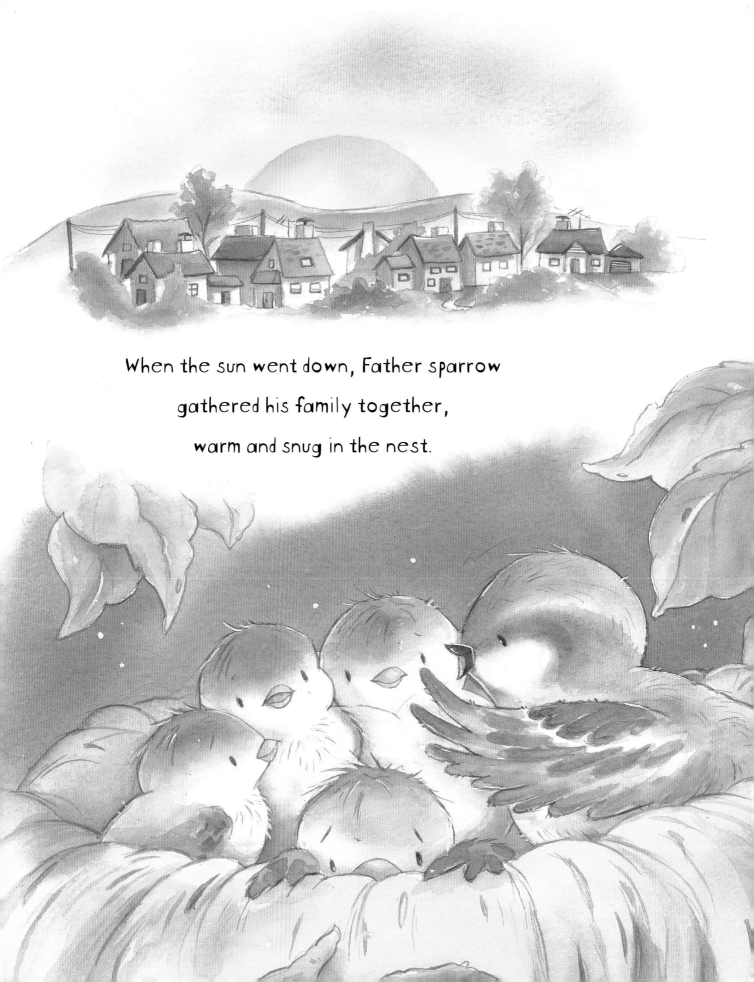

When the sun went down, Father sparrow
gathered his family together,
warm and snug in the nest.

He told them wonderful stories of long ago and far away:

of the Great Father who made the world and everything in it;

of how the day begins, and where the wind comes from, and all the little things that every creature knows.

The young birds listened with bright eyes.

But the Very Worried Sparrow peered out into the darkness. 'Meep,' he said, 'oh dear!'

When summer came, the Very Worried Sparrow
felt just a little braver. He set off with his
brothers and sisters to look for seeds in the field.
    SWOOSH!

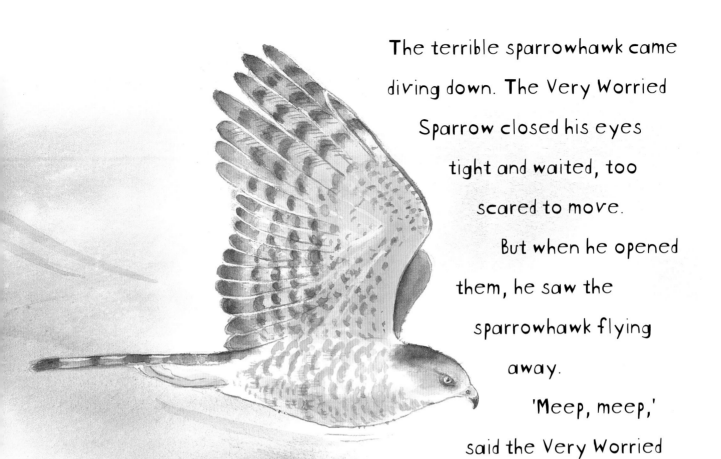

The terrible sparrowhawk came diving down. The Very Worried Sparrow closed his eyes tight and waited, too scared to move.

But when he opened them, he saw the sparrowhawk flying away.

'Meep, meep,' said the Very Worried Sparrow. 'I'm going home.' And he flew to the nest as fast as he could.

The autumn winds blew
and the trees shed their
leaves. Then the snow
fell, covering the ground in
a soft layer of sparkling white.
The sparrows thought it was wonderful.

The Very Worried Sparrow peered about him. 'The
snow has covered up all the food,' he said. 'And where
will we find water to drink?'

But each morning children scattered seeds
on the path and broke the ice that glazed the
pond. The sparrows had plenty to eat and drink
all through the winter.

Spring came and the sparrows twittered with excitement.

'It's nesting time,' they said.

They swooped and sang with all the other sparrows.

Soon pairs of birds were darting away, looking for safe places to build their nests.

'Meep, meep,' said the Very Worried Sparrow,
his head drooping. 'I'm all alone.'

The branch bounced as a little sparrow fluttered closer.

'Cheep,' she said shyly.

'Meep, meep,' said the Very Worried Sparrow.
'Will you be my friend?'

'Oh yes!' she said happily.

'I know a good place for a nest,' she said. 'Come and see.'

Together they flew to a lovely apple tree.

'Meep, meep,' said the Very Worried Sparrow. 'It's
lovely. But I expect other birds have found it already.'

'It's a safe place just for us,' chirruped his mate.
'Come on!'

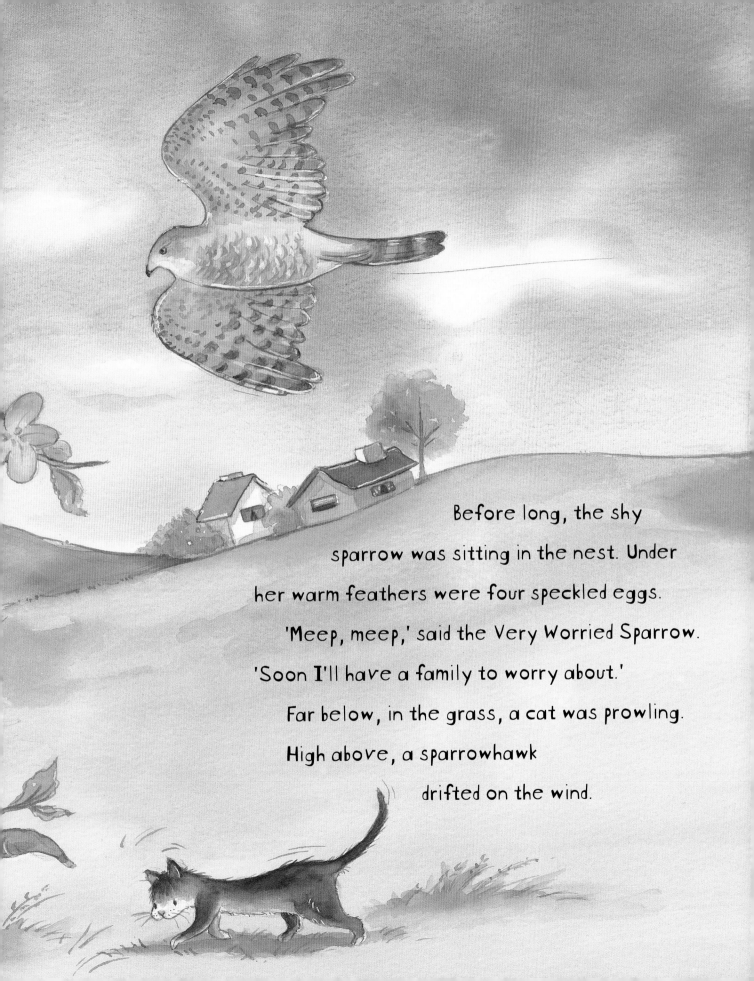

Before long, the shy
sparrow was sitting in the nest. Under
her warm feathers were four speckled eggs.
'Meep, meep,' said the Very Worried Sparrow.
'Soon I'll have a family to worry about.'
Far below, in the grass, a cat was prowling.
High above, a sparrowhawk
drifted on the wind.

The Very Worried Sparrow was
looking very, very... worried!

'Roo coo. What's the matter?' asked a gentle voice.

It was the turtledove with soft white feathers.

'I'm so worried,' wept the sparrow.

'Roo coo,' said the dove.

'Don't you know the stories of the Great Father who made us all and who cares about every sparrow?'

'Meep, meep,' said the Very Worried Sparrow.

'I was so worried, I didn't listen.'

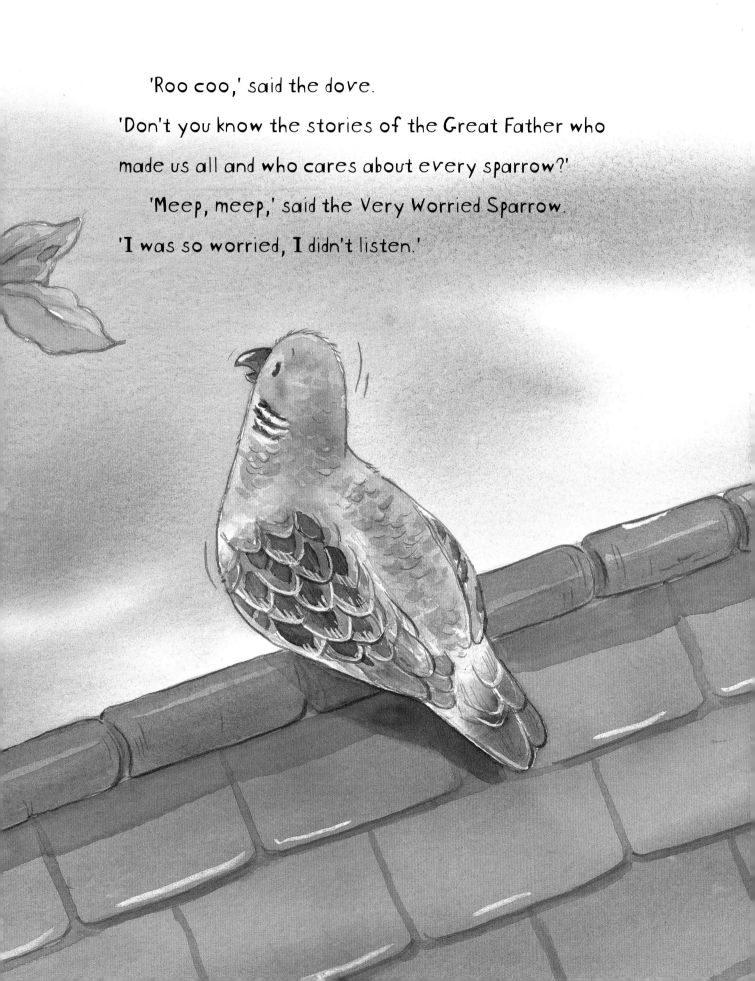

So, as the sun went down, the dove gathered all the birds around her, and told the stories of long ago and far away:

of the Great Father who made the world and everything in it;

of how the day begins, and where the wind comes from, and all the little things that every creature knows.

She spoke of the seasons and the years, of how things grow and new life comes. She told how the Great Father knows each creature and its time on the earth.

The next day, the whole world sparkled in the morning light.

'Tock, tock, tock.' A tiny sound came from each of the eggs, and soon four new baby sparrows hatched in the cosy nest.

Then the Very Worried Sparrow... smiled!

'I can't wait to
see them,' he said. 'We can
watch them grow and teach them to fly.
And I will tell them about the Great
Father who made the world and
everything in it, and who knows each sparrow. They won't have
to worry for a single day.'

Then the Very Worried Sparrow flew up into the blue sky.

'Cheep, cheep,' he sang, 'cheep, cheep, cheep,' loud
enough to burst with happiness.